Does A Snowflake Make A Sound?

Izaic Yorks

Ink & Virtue

First paperback edition November 23

Book design by Izaic Yorks

Editing by Courtney Yorks

ISBN 979-8-9873369-2-2 (paperback)

ISBN 979-8-9873369-6-0 (ebook)

www.IzaicYorks.com

Contents

Chapter 1: The Very Sudden And Quiet Passing Of Hanna Bear

Listen well, this is a tale of haunts and miracles, in a world much like our own. Except for the fact that it is an entirely flat world, housed in a glass pyramid, and swinging through the universe by a golden chain. Other than that, it is very much the same.

Understand?

If not, you need only to dispel your disbelief.

Our story begins with the death of Hanna Bear. It was December the fourteenth when Old Man Withers noticed something amiss and called the police. Alarms rang and lights lit *Snowcider Lane*—which was a rather dark, dead end, on account of its singular streetlight. The little elves carried out their little investigation, and after finding nothing amiss, called the coroner. So, he came. Driving up to the scene in his convertible, cherry bug, the troll lumbered into the rambler and declared: "No huntsman, magic, nor sunlight did this. Only the hands of time were at play here." Hanna had died in her sleep, alone (as ever she'd been) and peacefully. Then the little elves and the not-so-little coroner left, returning *Snowcider Lane* to its quiet solace.

"I always sit in that there chair and look out that there window. Seeing as her place is across from mine, I would often see her sweeping her steps. Well, one day I said to myself 'Withers Mathias Pettigrew, when was the last time you saw Hanna?' and just like the rest was history," Old Man Withers said to the local journalist, eager for a scoop (as nothing exciting ever happened in this little town).

Snowcider Lane was a particularly boring street, the kind only families and old people liked. It was the kind of place not even the snowplows came to, leaving it up to the residents to shovel whenever it did snow—partially because it was so far from downtown and also because there were only three households that occupied it (well, only two now). The street itself was arranged something like this: The Plicketts inhabited the four-story tower at the mouth of the street, then there were some woods, then at the end was Hanna's rambler and Old Man Wither's red barn shack.

As for Hanna Bear's funeral, she had no friends or relatives. Thus, the only people in attendance were funeral folk, Brother Casper and Tom (Mormon missionaries hard at work evangelizing the funeral folk), and a squirrel named Sir Mick-Nuts-A-Lot. To say the least, nobody cared, and nobody remembered, which Hanna was very bitter about. But as the Big Man would tell her, "It isn't anybody's fault but yours. . ."

Chapter 2: Hanna Goes To Heaven

"How was the bus trip?" asked The Big Man.

"A little stuffed, the poet was annoying and the ghosts entirely too spooky."

The Big Man chuckled. Although Hanna couldn't quite see him, because he was as bright as the glaring sun, she surmised his "gigantic*ness*" on account of the bellowing voice. Behind him was a pearly gate, and beyond that, nothing but stars. The Big Man asked his question once more, petting a cantankerous toad that lounged on the dais from which he had initially read her name.

Of all the things, why a toad? Hanna wondered.

"Get over it lady," ribitted the warty amphibian.

"Now that's not nice, Pharaoh," mused The Big Man. "You see Ms. Bear, It's always good to have a pestilence on hand. Besides, insects aren't the only thing that stick well to their tongues. A heavenly toad records Truth like no other. Now, let's see here. . . ah, yes. A wonderful life, a wonderful soul."

Hanna warmed considerably.

"But one problem that I'm afraid just won't stand," tutted The Big Man. "You missed the point of living. How were you supposed to love anyone by choosing a solitary life?"

Hanna's blood (not that she had any) ran cold. "I didn't choose it! I mean, I did, but look at how awful the world is. People are awful. You haven't any idea."

"Haven't I?"

Hanna's jaw clamped shut and she asked, "What do you mean to do?"

"Why send you back of course! As a ghost."

"But you say that those aren't good that they can't be—"

The Big Man clapped his hands and the heavens burst with wind. Hanna was flying away. Yanked by an invisible rope. The Big Man's words rumbled across time and space:

"And by what can't my grace achieve? *Snowcider Lane* yet has need of you. For your task, I will give you three gifts: You will not be bound to the place of your passing. You will be able to affect things of material. And into dreams you shall walk," echoed his voice, chased by the chirp of his toad.

Chapter 3: Danger Plickett Plays Ball

December 16th

Danger Plickett retrieved his ball, chased by the chirps of some angry bird he'd disturbed. Returning to the center of the yard he played under the shadow of Hanna's old house. It'd been nearly a year since the bear had passed away but her yard showed no sign of its missing mistress. This was on account of Danger's father who tended the yard, grumbling, "Keep on, keeping that property value." Unfortunately (yet another gripe of Mr. Plickett), every potential homebuyer had been chased off by something or another.

Pale as the moon some would say, scary as bloody mary others would whisper, one way or another it always ended in the words, "Ghost." Naturally, this had attracted all sorts of children to *Snowcider Lane,* looking for a glimpse of Hanna's spirit. Everyone saw something—*except* for Danger. To this day, Danger had never once encountered a thing. He'd spent nights in the drafty place, done stupid dares, and once tried more occult methods—none of it worked. Danger was convinced that everyone was in on some spectacular prank, one in which he was the butt of the joke. But hope lived on in the boy, and so he always played in Hanna's yard, praying that one day he'd see something spooky.

"Plickett comes to bat," Danger said, using his best announcer voice. "Remember folks! Nobody has ever seen him strike out. Home runs, all day." Danger threw the ball in the air and swung. *Miss!*

Retrieving the ball, he threw it up once again. "Home runs, all day!" *Miss.*

"Shoot! Shoot! Humans in a cauldron! Shoot!" Picking up the ball, Danger took a deep breath. *One more time. Come on, Danger! You got this.* "Home runs *all day*!" Tightening his green hands about the handle of the bat, he tossed the ball.

Up, up, up, went the ball, then down, down, down it came. Danger swung.

WHAPAM!

The ball flew through the oak trees, over the burbling creek, across the frosty road, and threw Old Man Withers's front window. Glass shattered and the word "PLICK-ET'" rose from the shack. Bursting through the stable doors galloped Old Man Withers. He ran across the road, leaped over the creek, and wove through the pillars of trees. Snatching Danger by the leg and hoisting him into the air, the centaur huffed in the goblin's face. "What in tarnation are you doing? You broke my window!" The horseman shook the boy scaring him really good. "If I ever catch you over here again, I promise you'll regret it! Now scram!" Danger scrambled away, never once looking back.

Danger didn't get that ball back anytime soon (soon, as it relates to *Prime Shipping* and download times, that is) and for a long time he didn't play in Hanna's yard (which for a boy of seven constitutes about a week), but he never did forget the smell on Old Man Withers's breath. The sickly-sweet scent of apple brandy was indelibly etched into his memory.

Neither he nor Old Man Withers noticed the faint outline of a bear in the old rambler window, as the spirit of Hanna watched on.

Chapter 4: Message in a Bottle

December 16th

Old Man Withers slurped a mouthful of the spirit—the drink warming him from chest to hooves. Stoking the fire, he found his usual seat (a rather smelly spot of hay next to the hearth) and admired everything about the brandy, from its sharp taste to its amber color, and even the vessel in which it was housed. The centaur's shack was filled with the empty bottles. It seemed a shame to throw away such beautiful glass work. Someone had spent a lifetime learning how to make these bottles—or so he told himself. He refused to imagine these works of art being churned out by some unfeeling machine.

Old Man Withers had no plans of getting drunk and hadn't since completing AA long ago. The rather large fairy who'd led the group had said an alcoholic could never go back: "One drink and the spiral will happen all over again." At first, Old Man Withers had been on board with it all, but in time he'd changed his mind. Moderation was the key to life. Why abstain when you could have a little of both worlds? Therefore, he'd made a new pact. No drinking before seven. The clock chimed nine.

"I done shown them," Old Man Withers said, starting to feel sufficiently relaxed. He liked it this way. Being drunk was bad, but not this. He'd once been told he was a sad drinker. But here, under the slight influence, he could withstand all things. Reaching across the coffee table, he grabbed the letter. One part urged him to take it to the postmaster, another to throw it in the fire, and the other to bury it out back. The latter thought seemed dramatic (it was) but was perfectly sensible under the influence. He set the letter back down and swished the bottle. Took another sip, and thought of his former wife. How long ago did they buy this place? It was to be halfway spot, while they built the farm of their dreams. How long ago had he chased her and his children away with all his work? One day they were together and the next they were divorcing. Of course, the courts had promised equal rights. But what does the state know of family politics? "You will see them, so long as you pay child support Mr. Pettigrew," had squawked the judge. Well, he did (worsening his workaholism), and yet he saw hardly a lick of his children—his ex made sure of that.

"But you were always waiting, weren't you, Mistress Brandy?" He took another sip. Before he knew it, he had drunk the bottle and was a crying mess. A roll of paper slipped between his teeth as he sucked out the last sips of the spirit. Wiping tearful eyes, he unfurled the waxy paper and eagerly read it (for some time ago, a clever executive had thought it would be a good idea to follow the fortune cookie model and slip notes in the bottom of the bottles. Most were poor attempts at dissuading alcoholics, but some were funny. Thus, in the end, it made everyone all the more excited to finish each and every bottle).

The note read:

If no one sees you eat the food, then it doesn't have calories.

Old Man Withers smiled. Truer words could not have been written. It was then in his self-induced haze, that he decided what to do with the letter. Grabbing the envelope, he stuffed it into the empty bottle. Then, turning on some wistful-sounding folk music he retrieved a new bottle of brandy from the cabinet, and ventured out back. It was a cool, starless night. Stiff grass crunched under hoof. Not a creature made a peep, and even the mosquitos couldn't be enticed to chase after the shirtless old centaur. Taking a rusty old shovel from the shed, he broke ground and buried the bottle, and the letter within. Then he uncorked the new bottle and slurped down the drink—hardly tasting a thing, only enjoying the nose-clearing burn.

"If no one sees you eat the food, then it doesn't have calories," Old Man Withers laughed.

Except, the ghost of Hanna did see and so she began to think and so she began to bake.

Chapter 5: Share a Pie, Make a Friend

December 23rd

"Darling," Mr. Plickett said, smoothing a perfectly oiled mustache and adjusting the grotesque top hat upon his head. Danger's father looked like something out of a Victorian story (and well should he, as the goblin was Prime Minister of the Goblins for the Victorian Revival Society) ."I hardly see why we should invite him. He gives me a bad feeling."

"The poor horse has no one, Herbert Plickett," chastised Danger's mother. Mrs. Plickett was in the midst of whipping up swamp soup (which, believe me, called for *actual* swamp water). Around them, their brood of children dashed this way and that, running with scissors, playing tag, and pretending to hunt humans. Of all the children, only Danger was a good boy—his heart was a little too big.

"But dear, we have enough mouths to feed, what with the guests coming and all—" One look from Mrs. Plickett and he gave up his protests. "Alright, if I must," Mr. Plickett grumbled, fumbling with his gold sutter tie. "Twenty-five years and I still can't tie a puffer right. If Grangeworth knew, I'd be the laughingstock of the society."

"He doesn't and I hardly think anyone really cares about your cosplay," Mrs. Plickett said. "Danger, your father is going to be a while. Why don't *you* go and invite Mr. Withers?"

"But Mom," Danger started.

"None of that son," Mr. Plickett snapped, "run along."

Grumbling, Danger ambled out of the tower, onto sunny *Snowcider Lane,* where then he trudged to Old Man Withers's place.

Walking up to the paint-peeling door, Danger was just about to clang the impish gargoyle knocker, when he sniffed something delicious. Across the way, on Hanna's windowsill sat a freshly steaming pie. Danger's mouth watered at the smell of caramelized apples, baked in butter and cinnamon. He might have left it alone, if not for the congregate of crows assembling along the bare oak branches. Jumping the creek (now running reverse due to the swing of the world. By mid-afternoon, when the world swung the other direction, the water would run the other way), Danger tiptoed up the creaky steps and said, "Hello? You left your pie out. The crows will eat it soon."

In response the door to the house whined softly as the wind pushed it slightly ajar, giving Danger the proper heebie-jeebies, but otherwise, no response was forthcoming. Frowning, the little goblin ran to the windows (those he could reach) and peered within. Dark and dark. Cold and cold. There wasn't a chance anyone had been in the house.

Shrugging, Danger scooped up the pie (as any child would) and marveled at his good fortune. The pie was piping hot still and none of the proper questions came to the goblin's thick skull. Instead, he skipped back to Old Man Withers's place, singing jollily all the way. "Precious, precious, my precious humble pie. I'm gonna eat ya and hide ya in my drawer!"

"I done told you not to come around, Plickett," was all Withers said at Danger's knock. The little goblin almost left, but he knew Mrs. Plickett would not take no for an answer. So more out of fear for himself he pushed the issue.

"But sir, we wanted to invite you over for Yule dinner. There'll be good food and desserts. Mom makes a killer Yule log."

Old Man Withers squinted at Danger for some time. He was all gruff and grizzle, much like a threadbare carpet after years of use. "Is that apple pie with raisins?" Old Man Withers asked, pointing at the treat.

"Oh well, I don't know." Danger said, not liking the hungry look in the old horseman's eye. "A friend gave it to me. All mine you see." Old Man Withers licked his lips, giving a long, deflated look. At first, Danger was proud to see how effectively his lie worked. The centaur looked so sad, and the goblin only felt shame.

"You can have a bite, I suppose," Danger mumbled. Crossly, he offered up the tin. He needn't say anymore. Old Man Withers didn't even bother with cutlery (and why should he? He is a horseman after all) but thrust his face straight into the platter. Pie stuff splattered everything, and everyone close by.

"Hey! Hey!" Danger snarled, showing the points of saw-like teeth. "That's mine—" but Old Man Withers, nickered and neighed over anything the little boy had to say.

"Dangum, it's the same! The same! But how could you have known?" Then, seriously, the centaur shook the boy as if that would extract the information he desired. "Where did you get this recipe? Who told it to you?"

"I just found the pie," Danger stuttered. He must have sounded truly frightened, for Old Man Withers set him down with a swift apology. "Sorry boy! I just haven't had that in so long," he said, wiping his tears away. "A Yule dinner? Done. I'll be there."

Without a further word, he shut the door in Danger's face. The goblin blinked, looking at the empty pie tin, the gargoyle knocker, then his shoe—upon which he spied a final chunk of pie. *Some pie is better than no pie*, Danger shrugged. Unhinging his jaw, he let the coils of his tongue loose. The pink muscle slithered down, wrapped up the pie, and then rolled back into his wretched mouth. Danger swallowed without chewing once. It tasted of ash but it smelled just fine (only human flesh actually had flavor to a goblin, but these were civilized goblins and had thus given up any such barbarism. It should be noted, that goblins simply love to eat. It could be a dunghill for all they cared. The thought of eating alone is enough to excite any one of the miscreants). Skipping home, Danger Plickett sang *Silent Night* (a particular goblin favorite all about the fall of Moria) failing to notice the last curls of smoke rising from Hanna's chimney.

Chapter 6: A Proper Plickett Panegyric

December 23rd

Everyone was silent.

Mr. Plickett's guests were patiently quiet on account that it was the proper Victorian thing to do. All of the goblin and hobgoblin guests were dressed for the soiree in the height of nineteenth-century fashion.

The Plickett children suffered their father's long-winded speech, on the threat of the switch, and an hour without their phones.

Mrs. Plickett was meek, because she was a crunchy mom, and had nothing better to do than wonder whether or not her guests would recycle or repent of their gas-guzzling cars (she had made sure to virtue signal the point by not only putting up one sign in the yard, but five hundred. Those signs were silent on account of them being only layers of paper, which Mrs. Plickett would later throw away. I digress, why doesn't anybody ever ask what a tree wants to be? Maybe they don't want to be paper. A survey should be conducted. But I suppose that would require some paper).

Old Man Withers was silent because he had spied the alcohol, and it was almost seven.

Hanna went unheard because, well, she was a ghost.

Only Mr. Plickett wasn't silent, on account of the speech he was giving in preparation for the darkest nights of the year.

"Gentle goblins and goblinas and friends of ours, it is a pleasure to have you all gathered here," Mr. Plickett said, speaking like a great tubby man, with a great tubby voice. All of the Plickett clan groaned, but they knew better than to correct his "regal" Victorian personae.

"As we move into the last days of the year, let us renew our faith on the return of the sun. Let us place hopes in the good of the coming day. And let us bind the ties that tie the binds upon our bound kinship (everyone looked confused at that, giving an odd, dispassionate clap). But first, before the revelry and the pipes (the mention of the favored tobacco pastime drew a much more fervent *Here! Here!* from amongst the Victorian party), let us look to the symbols of the eve. Danger, Mucus, Wartbum, if you would?" Leaping to their feet, all three goblins bustled into the motions of the much-rehearsed affair.

Danger, the smallest of the three, fetched the pale candle. "To represent the return of the light," Mr. Plickett said, lighting the taper.

"Sourced local," screeched Mrs. Plickett, which the candle was—direct from the coroner's ear.

Mucus returned, strewing lengths of human hair in the hearth. "To cleanse away ghosts and spirits," Mr. Plickett announced.

"Straight from the town cancer clinic," squawked Mrs. Plickett, "support local!"

Last but not least came Wartbum. The eldest goblin was a bodybuilding brute and had no problem hoisting the little tree. "Thank you," Mr. Plickett beamed, using a saw to cut off the end of the tree. "Through the course of this night, we shall burn this for warmth. A reminder that all we need is provided and there is plenty to share."

"Burn it," Mrs. Plickett cheered as her husband began the yule fire. "always burn local!"

"Let us feast, smoke, and have a Yule bash," Mr. Plickett roared, once the fire was at proper blaze. Chaos erupted in the form of cheers and darting bodies. The Victorians rushed to gather their pipes and strolling shoes—there was still time for lunting. The children raced for the food and control of the music. And Old Man Withers, seeing the clock strike seven, made his way to the bar. There was a plastic bowl with a pink concoction. A bevy of brews. And goblin wine, which he wrote off immediately, knowing the stuff to be composed of aged barley and spit. There was nothing to his taste. He was disappointed, to say the least.

"Good thing I brought you," Old Man Withers whispered to himself. From the flap of his patchy tweed jacket, he retrieved a little silver flask. He had barely twisted open the battered top when Mrs. Plickett said: "I'm so glad you came—Oh, what do you have there?"

"This? Ah, it ain't nothing. Just a little something I always done carry." Shame filled him, and wonderment at whether she knew or not? Could they see him for the alcoholic he was? When she held out her hand Old Man Withers was reluctant to give it over.

Removing the top, she gave it a sniff. "Apple Brandy?"

Old Man Withers shrugged.

"Silly horse, you should have just asked. My husband keeps all sorts of stuff for his cosplaying friends."

"Cosplay?" Old Man Withers asked.

"Pretending to be something you're not, you know, that sort-a-thing. Now, I'll bet you three nails and a roach that we have the exact thing in his office. Give me a moment." Before he could say *neigh* the goblina was gone. Old Man Withers sighed in relief. She didn't know. No one knew. *Cosplay, huh, I can do that too.* "I'll keep at a social level," Old Man Withers promised himself. It would be strange to drink nothing at all, and just as bad to drink entirely too much.

"Here you are," Mrs. Plickett said, returning to hand him a full bottle of Apple Brandy.

"What am I supposed to done do with this?"

"Drink some and share some. What else?"

"Yes well, umm, I meant without a cup," Old Man Withers said sheepishly, kicking gently at the floor.

"Shave a fish and stuff my gullet," Mrs. Plickett cursed, "silly me." Finding him a cup, she smiled and said, "I am so glad you came."

"Thanks for inviting me. It's been some time since I've been around a family. It's really. . . nice. And that apple pie, I do declare was divine."

Mrs. Plickett raised an eyebrow—the question obvious on her face.

"The apple raisin one, Mrs. Plickett. My old woman used to make those, the last time I tasted it was a few weeks before our first was born." He fell silent, a sudden pang in his heart. Pouring himself a large glass of brandy, he threw back a mouthful of the stuff. The burn was weak, but it would have to do. Swallowing, Old Man Withers remembered just where he was and weakly said, "It's very good."

Mrs. Plickett nodded slowly, "I didn't make any sort of pie, but I do make a Yule log that is to die for. Mr. Withers how long have you been alone—"

But before the centaur could answer there was a crash and cackle of laughter. Five of the Plickett children were swinging from the chandeliers and one had just fallen onto the table. Gravy and porcelain scattered everywhere.

"Not the bone china!" Mrs. Plickett howled, chasing after her children. "Scuttle! You get back here! I swear, you're gonna live like one of them Amish children! This is *your* offspring, Herbert Plickett!" Unfortunately, the goblin patriarch was nowhere to be seen, as he had left to march up and down the street with his brigade of Victorian, pipe-loving friends.

Left all alone, Old Man Withers looked at the little green bottle. *Smiling Orchard.* It wasn't his favorite brand, but it would do.

Now, Mr. Plickett wasn't completely alone, because Hanna's ghost was never too far. In fact, after a terrible degree of effort, she had managed to unzip the shoulder bag he'd brought (no small task, mind you, seeing as a ghost hasn't any mass).

"You brought my ball back," Danger said, drawn to the centaur, spying it in his bag.

Old Man Withers choked on his drink, surprised to see the bottle nearly drained. Hiding it behind his back, he set down his cup and handed over the toy. "Well, it done didn't seem right," the centaur said, already feeling the creeping buzz. *Did anyone else notice the happy haze about the room?* He blinked the thought away. "It's my favorite," Danger said, glad to have his ball back. Turning it, he showed Old Man Withers the golden signature upon it: *Itchy Ro*

"See! The world's greatest ball player. I don't care nothin' anyone else says."

For his part, Old Man Withers had to agree, seeing as he wasn't a fan of sports—they were too boisterous for his tastes.

"Old Man Withers. . ."

"Yes, Plickett?"

"Sorry for busting your window."

"You should be," Old Man Withers huffed, then more softly, and after some thought, he added, "Son, I'm sorry for taking it. And I'm awfully glad you invited me here. It's been a time since I was around a family." His eyes grew damp at the edges, and he didn't realize he'd been drinking until he finished the brandy. *Cosplay,* Withers thought, *darn it all to tarnation. I don't have problems. Cosplay!* But everything in the old centaur broke when Danger gave him a quick little hug.

Filled with a swirl of emotion, Old Man Withers coped only as he knew how.

"Damn the dang cosplay!" taking the entire grog bowl he drank every lost drop and fled from the house. Danger tried to follow, only to be caught by the arms of his mother.

Pushing past Mr. Plickett and his gang of pretenders, chased by Mrs. Plickett's confused cries, Old Man Withers galloped for home. Slamming the door behind him, he collapsed on the floor. Cold and lonely. Well, except for his mistress. Undoing the flask, he enjoyed the brandy but not for the taste.

Hanna watched and called the ambulance; though it was not the first time she had done this; it was the first time she was determined to make a difference in his life.

Chapter 7: The Horse Who Drank Too Much

December 23rd

Old Man Withers lived. Saved by the pump. It had been an uncomfortable experience, but he supposed that was better than dead. Outside the sun was just beginning to rise. "You sure you got someone at home to keep an eye on you?" asked the doctor's assistant.

"I'll be just fine," Old Man Withers grunted, taking extra care not to look her in the face—just in case. The hospital doors hissed wide as he left. Braving the cold, he hailed a taxi.

"You reek, man," said the cabbie. "Just so we're straight, should you throw up, my cleaning fee starts at one hundred and twenty pounds."

"Just drive."

"Fine, where to boss," said the driver.

"844 Snowcider Lane." Then, to himself, he grumbled, "What dang person hires a Medusa to work at the hospital."

"What's that?" asked the driver.

"Just drive," Old Man Withers scowled.

"Fine, fine." The driver said. Twiddling the dial, he found a station to his liking and bumped the music. Bollywood love songs blared in the cab. Old Man Withers could only take it for so long.

"Would you turn down that racket!"

"Fine, fine," frowned the driver. He turned it off. Only the sounds of the cab remained, its hybrid engine whirring like some great big toy. The driver shifted. Leather rubbed over plastic. *Dangun mouth breather,* Old Man Withers thought, listening to the man breathe. Old Man Withers looked at the driver's GPS. *Twenty-four minutes. Stupid phones never know the fastest ways, and kids these days don't know how to find a thing without them.* He almost told the man to hang a left on *Shady Grove* but decided against it. He would rather suffer a longer drive in silence than a shorter one in conversation. *Maybe I'll just close my eyes.*

Eee-er-ee-er-ee-er-ee—

"What is that racket?" Old Man Withers exclaimed.

"Huh? This? It's my guardian angel."

"Why does it have a done dere bobble-head? That's stupid."

"My son gave it to me," said the man.

"Well give it back," Old Man Withers said under his breath, not realizing that the cabbie could hear him.

"I think not, good sir. My son would be mighty disappointed if I did. I come here from upstate because the tips are better, but the roads along the way are treacherous. I've never seen so many accidents before moving here—"

"What are you talking about?" Old Man Withers snapped. "You don't have them road laws where you're from. I heard that even chickens and other things walk all about."

The cabbie should've been offended, but he wasn't. "Contraire," piped the man. "That's a misunderstanding. The chickens actually direct the traffic, and they rarely cluck it up. Anyways, see this little angel here?"

Eee-er-ee-er-ee-er-ee—

"I *hear* that little angel *there.*"

"It's a promise to my family that I'll be safe. That I'll be home for Christmas and every day before and after."

Old Man Withers snorted.

"You laugh but surely you understand? Don't you have anyone waiting at home for you?"

"Would I be coming from a stomach pump if I did?"

The cabbie was quiet a moment, and then, upon pulling into Old Man Withers's lot, he declared: "I've just the thing."

"Yeah? Well, hurry it up. You have until I finish swiping my card."

The driver fumbled in the glove box, a strange mix of smells unfurling from the compartment. Roasted peanuts and old fish sauce.

"It better not be your lunch," the centaur said, pinching his nose.

"Breakfast. And it isn't." Leaning back, the driver handed him an old tape cassette. "I was given this by a fellow on the tube a week ago. I was minding my business when a sharp-dressed man, maybe a broker or something, came up to me. I'll never forget his bowler cap; it was the brightest green you've ever seen. He called me by name, which was strange, seeing as we had never met before. And he gave me this. Said I'd know what to do with it when the time came. I tried to protest, but the tube came to a stop, and he disappeared into the crowd of people, all pushing to get to their daily affairs. Well, I think it's meant for you."

Old Man Withers thought the entire affair to be rather queer and so he didn't say much (plus he was too tired to protest). Instead, the centaur accepted the tape cassette and climbed out of the cab.

Old Man Withers watched as the cabbie pulled away. Goosebumps prickled his skin as he watched the red-tail lights grow smaller and smaller, before turning out of sight. He slapped his face. *Surely, I'm done mistaken?* But Old Man Withers knew what he'd seen as the taxi pulled away. That stupid bobbled head. Shaking, always shaking. Had it not been dressed like some businessman? Its head, capped by a green, if faded, bowler. Old Man Withers shook his head and decided he was being entirely too superstitious. "I'm tired and that's that." Entering his home he took one last look at the cabbie's gift, reading the title of it aloud. "Screw? Strange." Throwing it aside, Old

Man Withers collapsed into his hay, falling into an uneasy sleep.

Chapter 8: Danger's Dream

December 23rd

Danger begrudgingly went to sleep. Clutching his baseball, he sullenly snuggled into his bed—a hamper hanging on the wall by a hook.

"He's a drunk," Danger said, mocking the tone his mother had used. "Stay away from him."

"Go to sleep, Danger," rebuked his brother, Bilgerat. His sibling lay sprawled out below Danger's nest, preferring the cold hardstone to his bed. His saucer-sized eyes looked up at Danger, glowing in the dark.

"Just cause he gave your ball back doesn't mean much. It was yours after all," Bilgerat said. Danger stuck out his tongue. He didn't expect his brother to understand. Bilgerat hadn't seen just how sad Old Man Withers had been. Before this evening, Danger had never seen an adult cry. He didn't like it. Danger knew what cheered him up when he was sad. *Paper airplanes made by friends. Chocolate cake from Mr. Dungbeetle's bakeshop. Someone to give me a hug.* Rolling in his dirty hamper, he nuzzled into the fetid sheets. A fly buzzed about. Catching it with a flick of the tongue, he chewed the treat thoughtfully. *What can I do?* But Danger was just a boy, and his mother would skin him alive if she caught him over there. She'd done that once to Kitty, whose skin had never quite grown back right.

But there was nothing to be done, and so he went to sleep.

Danger blinked. He was in a dream (not that he realized). Looking around he thought himself to be lost in the woods, but then he realized he was in Old Man Withers's backyard. The sound of a spade striking soil and rock caught the goblins' attention.

"What are you doing?" Danger asked. But Old Man Withers ignored him, seemingly unable to see him. The centaur worked to dig a hole. His movements were strangely lethargic, and upon smelling the brandy, Danger knew he was drunk.

"No hope, none whatsoever," Old Man Withers slurred. Pulling something from his jacket, the centaur dropped it into the hole. As Old Man Withers filled the hole, Danger walked about, trying to get a better look at what it was. A bottle with a little letter stuffed inside. Then, it was covered by a shovel full of dirt. Then another. And another, until only a gentle mound remained.

"There," Old Man Withers said, wavering back and forth. "Ain't never gonna be a Christmas where I get what I want." Tossing the shovel into an overgrown bush, the centaur wiped his eyes. "Miracles done be for the dead."

Then walking back into the warmth of his abode, he slammed the door shut behind him.

Danger scratched his head.

"So that's it? Santa ain't just for kids! Don't worry Old Man Withers!" And like that, Danger awoke, remembering everything he'd seen—except the bear, who'd watched everything unfold to her design.

Bilgerat snored like a chainsaw, rattling Danger's sleepies away. He felt inspired. More than ever, Danger knew he needed to help Old Man Withers. *I gotta go find out what's got Old Man Withers in knots. But mom said I can't.* Danger sucked on his lip, turning it from green to pink. He thought of the dreadful fruit knife. Just thinking of it hurt. But doing nothing hurt even more (his heart was too many times large for a goblin after all). *If I don't get caught, I don't get skinned.* Simple enough.

Clutching his baseball (it went everywhere with him), Danger crept down the wall, tip-toed over his brother, lurked through the door, stalked down the hall, avoided catdog (stitched together by his father's own hand), waddled down the stairs, and was almost to the door when she spoke.

"Dan'er what you doin?"

"Apocalypse!" Danger hissed at his youngest sister. She looked pathetic, all sleepy-eyed, in her footie pajamas and with a stuffie in hand. "What do you want?"

"I was hungry."

"Never sneak up on a goblin, Apocalypse. You might get hurt. Jeez, you could have scared the poop out of me."

"Is that why you pee'd?" Apocalypse yawned, pointing to the wet spot on his trousers.

Danger flushed.

"I was going to pee outside, thank you."

"Why? We have a bat'room."

"I like the feel of the wind. You wouldn't understand, Apocalypse. Now, go back to bed."

His little sister shrugged and started for the steps, only to stop and tilt her little head. "Mama said we can't go out."

"Yeah," Danger said, pulling open the door, "what she doesn't know won't hurt her."

Apocalypse didn't look too sure.

"I'll tell her and then she'll s'in you."

"You wouldn't," Danger snarled, but one look at the goblina and he knew she would (they were siblings after all).

"Fine! How about a deal? I'll give you anything, so long as you go back to bed and forget you saw me leaving."

"Anyting?"

"Anything."

Apocalypse hardly mused it over. "I want Icky Ro."

Danger was aghast. "No. Not ever, ever, ever. Pick something else."

His sister's lips formed into a pout and she scraped the claws of her feet along the floor. "Moooom, Mooooom," she started.

Danger's heart began to beat super-fast. He almost called it off but remembered just how sad and alone Old Man Withers had been.

"Fine, Apocalypse. Here, take it! If I find it cleaned, even a little, I will personally put you in the stockade." Handing over the ball he shivered at the goblina's wicked giggle. Sing-song, Apocalypse said, "Icky, Icky, Icky Ro, bath time, teatime, sweet time ro."

"It's *Itchy* Ro," Danger whispered fiercely, but his sister was already running up the steps as fast as she could.

Swallowing hard, Danger snuck from his home and down *Snowcider Lane.* There was only one streetlight, but tonight the light of the moon sufficed. It was cold—the promise of snow just on the horizon. Danger wished he had brought a jacket and shoe. Oh well.

Coming to Old Man Withers's home, he found it dark within. Only the smallest embers in the centaur's hearth remained as a bastion against the night. On the tips of his toes, he looked through the windows.

Old Man Withers was sound asleep, on his side, his brandy just out of reach. Danger nodded. Made sense. *Some people sleep with stuffies, I sleep with Itchy Ro, and others with bottles.* Remembering why he'd come, Danger wandered to the back. It was exactly as he had seen it, even the mound of dirt was there—if frostier than in his dream. Looking about, he found the spade in the same bush. Plucking a cockroach from the handle, he proceeded to unearth what Old Man Withers had buried.

Not too long after, Danger dusted off a dirty bottle and pulled free the letter from within. It was crinkled and needed some smoothing. Though he couldn't read it he knew it exactly for what it was. "A letter to Santa," Danger smiled. "Don't worry Old Man Withers, you might have been a bad boy, but I've been an angel. There's no way Santa can turn *me* down." Tucking the letter under his arm, Danger was halfway down *Snowcider Lane* when remembered to return all the things the way they'd been.

Running back, he filled the hole and tossed the spade into the brush. Then, at last, ready to be warm and snug, he returned home.

Never once did Danger notice the ghost behind him, whispering in his ear.

The next day, the postman came to collect the mail including the letter Danger had retrieved.

"You sure this is for Santa," grumbled the woman, rubbing her beard (it's a curse all dwarves must suffer, from infants to women). "I can read!" was all Danger said.

"Yup," was all the postman replied, for she was far too busy to argue with a goblin. "It'll get delivered."

Chapter 9: Screwtape

December 24th

"*I will understand,*

(Hope of deliverance)
I will understand,
(Hope of deliverance). . ."

The music faded away. Old Man Withers wished he could have met Paul McCartney. He considered the man to be a right-round genius. Old Man Withers also wished to meet his own children. He wondered what they thought of him. *Doesn't matter. Wishes are for foals and fools.* Pouring himself a cup of coffee, the centaur popped out the cassette and snapped it back into its case. He was just about to make himself breakfast when he saw the gift from the cabbie. Picking up the little cassette tape he read it aloud. "Screw? A gift for me, huh?" Now Old Man Withers was no great believer in providence, *but* he did like his music, and the curiosity of what the little tape held within was too much to ignore.

"What the heck," Old Man Withers neighed. Popping it into the entertainment center he pressed play. At first, only the sound of rumbles and scratches came from the speakers. Grainy and distorted. Disappointed, Old Man Withers nearly pressed stop when the first real sound finally blared. It was not music but words. A sermon perhaps? No. A gameshow? No. Just a man talking? No.

Why, it was a centaur, and one Old Man Withers knew, very, very well.

The first voice belonged to him.

"What sort of devilish prank is this?" Old Man Withers asked, choking on his coffee. The strangeness had only begun. The voice from the cassette player was in a heated debate—*with his old woman.* "I've heard this argument," Old Man Withers breathed, "I made this argument." Knees quaking, he fell to the floor, listening as his ex pleaded for his attention. Pleaded for his presence in their marriage. But he shrugged her off with years of empty promises and gifts.

It was not just his viewpoint that he heard but that of his ex's as well. He heard her thoughts and the way she normalized his workaholism. He heard her hopes when she carried their children. *Maybe now my Withers will choose family*, she foolishly thought. Of course, she'd been wrong. *Why wasn't I there?* Old Man Withers lamented (of course, he knew the answer well enough). A childhood of poverty had driven him to provide for his family. "Why can't she see? Women are blind as they come," stormed his past self. But for the first time, Old Man Withers was the one who truly saw. He heard the pain in her mourning, in her affair, and in their divorce. Money, oats, and apples were a poor substitute for the man himself.

The tape unfurled his life. The tape gutted out his heart. When the end credits came it was without words, accompanied only by the sound of a lonely creek. He hardly heard the laughter as the tape rattled to an end—cruel and otherworldly. By then, Old Man Withers had drunk nearly the whole pot of coffee, lacing it with increasingly liberal doses of whiskey.

Too stunned for tears, Old Man Withers looked blearily at the clock: Seven in the morning. His AA group had told him alcoholism was a disease, something that couldn't be controlled—try as he might. "It only takes one thing to open the durned gates of hell," Withers blithered. He looked at the spirits clenched in either hand and made his decisions with a surprising amount of alacrity. They said his disease was incurable, so why try to fight it? He had no answer, deciding he'd wasted too much time, trying all those years prior to stave off the inevitable. He'd only lived a wretched life, extended against a predestined fate. *Best to lean in. At least I'll go happy.* Of course, in this case, "happy" meant numb.

Grabbing an armful of alcohol, Old Man Withers threw open the door. Without bothering for his jacket, he embarked out into the chilling day. It was a dull day, grey and melancholy. Heading out back, walking a short way through the woods he found a spot next to the pleasant little creek. Settling down, he laid out his liquid treasures, just as the first snowflakes began to fall—breaking silently upon the frosted ground. "A white Christmas," he said, "should be nice." Old Man Withers had no intention of seeing the day. Raising the bottle to his lips he gurgled down the burning drink. Between the bingeing and thoughtless doldrums, he watched the accumulating snow about him and wondered if a snowflake made a sound when it crashed into the earth. He couldn't hear a thing, but Hanna, ever near, certainly did. Wrapping her big bear arms around him she kept the worst of the cold at bay.

Chapter 10: A Christmas Miracle

December 24th

Interlocking arms, the Plickett family caroled their hearts out. They went from street to street and even took part in the town's janky Christmas parade. There were many things that the Plickett family was, but most of all they were a family of singers. Not the annoying kind, who randomly breaks out into songs, usually taken from children's movies (band nerds, you know I'm talking to you). The Plickett's were the family who sang when it was appropriate, and Christmas caroling was always appropriate!

So, it was with happy hearts and cold toes that the Plicketts returned to *Snowcider Lane.* "Wonderful job, my brood," extolled Mr. Plickett, as Mrs. Plickett collected the signs she had invariably hung from her children's necks; Mrs. Plickett's signs were all disconnected from the caroling, having something to do with: lives, nature, The Science, and *Stop Santa: Sleigh pulling is animal cruelty, use the humans instead.* "Yes! Yes!" Mrs. Plickett clapped. "Wonderful little billboards—I mean singers." And of course, the children were glad to be back, on account of the promise of hot chocolate—well, everyone was happy except for Danger, that was. The little goblin couldn't stop looking down the road at Old Man Withers's dark home—stark against the rising slopes of snow.

"Can't we just do one more?" Danger asked. "For Old Man Withers. He is all alone," he added when his parents asked whom it was they could've forgotten. Mr. and Mrs. Plickett had not forgotten the centaur but had purposefully ignored him—both certain of his flawed character. But it was Christmas Eve and when Danger added, "I won't ask for anything tomorrow or next year. Just one song to bring him cheer." Exchanging looks, his parents gave a sigh, and his father tussled his sprig of hair, saying, "It couldn't hurt." Mrs. Plickett, however, was slower to soften her heart, but a word from Mr. Plickett and she was screaming for the children to grab their signs and light their candles. Thus, the Plickett family jaunted merrily down that lonely road.

Coming to the front of the house, some questioned if he was even home, and others thought he was asleep, but still they sang.

They left four carols later, when not a light came on, and all remained silent in the house.

"Tried our best," Mr. Plickett said.

"Likely drunk as skunk operating a starship in a funk," sniffed Mrs. Plickett.

The children, for their part, sprinted ahead, each screaming first dibs at the hot cocoa—well, all but Danger that was.

"I forgot something," Danger told his father.

"And what could that be?" Mr. Plickett asked.

"*Err* my sock," Danger offered with an awkward little shrug.

Pursing his lips, Mr. Plickett finally nodded, whispering so only Danger might hear. "Your heart is too big for a goblin, Danger. You can look in the windows but don't go into the house. I'll tell your Mother you forgot your sign."

"Thank you, thank you!" giving his father a quick little hug, the goblin ran back to that lonely barn shack.

"Old Man Withers," Danger called, knocking on the door. He nearly jumped when it opened. It hadn't been closed all the way. "Hello? Did you hear us singing? We just wanted to wish you a Merry Christmas tomorrow!" There was no answer. Remembering his father's words, Danger nearly left, and would've if not for the sound of a cell phone. Standing at the door, he could see its neon green glow from where it buzzed on the table. Licking his lips, Danger waited to see if Old Man Withers would suddenly appear to answer it. No one came. The phone fell silent. Danger almost left. The phone rang again. Puffing out his chest, Danger stood just a bit taller and mustered every ounce of confidence in his little green body. Retrieving the phone, he ran back outside as fast as he could manage.

"There! I was only inside for a second. No worries," Danger said. "Now, who's calling at this hour?"

Unknown Number.

The phone stopped ringing. It was too bad Danger didn't know the password, because then he might listen to the voicemail. For the third time in a row, the phone began to ring.

"Old Man Withers!" Danger called. "I think someone really wants to talk." No answer. "Guess I tried." Danger was about to return the phone and head home when he saw something strange. Fresh in the snow were great big footprints. Tilting his head, he could see they led behind the house and into the forest beyond. The call went to voicemail and then the phone began to ring all over again. A strange and bizarre notion settled upon little Danger. Perhaps, Santa was calling, and perhaps these tracks would take him to Old Man Withers.

Following the tracks, Danger never once questioned just how big they were, nor that they looked something like bear prints (for boys are foolish). Instead, he delved into the forest and by the light of the moon found Old Man Withers snoring by the side of the creek. He looked almost peaceful though he reeked of spirits.

"Old Man Withers?" Danger asked. When the centaur didn't answer he proceeded to poke him. When that didn't work, he bit him on the rump. That worked.

"Tarnations!" Old Man Withers roared, leaping to his feet. Blinking the centaur seemed a bit confused to be in the woods and even more confused to see the little goblin holding his phone. The centaur flushed. "Plickett," Old Man Withers said, "what're you done doing here?"

"We came caroling and when you didn't come out, I got worried. Then I heard your phone, and I shouldn't have, but I grabbed it, because, well look, I think Santa's calling you."

"Ha!" Old Man Withers said caustically, snatching his phone. "Ain't Santa or no one ever cared about me for a long time. "

"I care for you."

"Cause you're a child. I've treated you horribly, remember?"

"I know. . . but doesn't mean I have to do the same to you."

Old Man Withers snorted, glaring at the boy. Danger fiddled with his fingers and kicked at the snow fluff. The phone rang again.

"Say's unknown, it's spam," Old Man Withers spat.

"They keep calling. You should answer."

"I should throw it in the creek is what I should durn do."

"Please! It's the sixth time, Old Man Withers," Danger pleaded (for by now he was exceptionally curious if it was the man in red).

"Will you stop bothering me and go home if I do?"

Danger nodded eagerly.

"Fine." Tapping the little green button, Old Man Withers answered the phone. "Hullo, Withers Pettigrew speaking."

There was a pause and Old Man Withers nearly hung up, thinking it a prank, but a hesitant voice rippled through the speaker:

"Dad? It's me, Seabiscuit Pettigrew. I got your letter. . ."

***

December 25th

So it was that for the first time in years, Old Man Withers connected with his children. It was the first time in years that his barn hut sparkled with Christmas lights and joy. And in later years he would come to not only celebrate all Christmases with his children, but also with the Plickett family—who came to adopt him as an honorary goblin (he also became a cosplayer, and was exceptionally gifted in the rarely practiced art of lunting, but that is an incredibly boring story that should never be told). Strangely, it should be noted, that when the centaur remembered that odd gift from the cabbie, he found the black tape cassette cracked and broken. The tape within was pulled out and screwed into a ruinous mess.

He never did discover who had done that.

***

December 25th

Contented, Hanna settled into the haunt of her home. Had she done enough? Was the Big Man watching? Who knew? Hanna had done the Good and that was well enough. From her window she watched the flicker of the firelight emanating from Old Man Withers's home, happiness swelling within her incorporeal chest. She was preparing to head into stasis (a pretend sleep for ghosts, it makes them feel somewhat normal, you understand) when a sound came from the chimney. A heavy scuffle, shuffle, and slumping thump. Soot and ash (left by the teenagers who would use the hearth when sleeping over, looking for a spook) sprayed about.

Hanna rubbed her eyes, disbelieving what she beheld. Dressed in a long tunic, cardinal red, thin, and with a trailing white beard, was a jolly man.

"Santa?" Hanna asked, "How could this be?"

"Ho! Ho! Ho! I prefer Saint Nicholas, or Nick should you like, and I could ask you the same question. But I won't, I just follow the guidance of the Big Man" he said, pointing up.

Hanna floated for joy.

"Does that mean, I'm free? My duty is done?"

Saint Nicholas shrugged, rustling through a great big bag that he pulled from a teensy-weensy pocket.

"Dunno, but the Big Man had me make something extra special for you." Holding up a metal disk, he inserted an elegant key into it and began to crank. Once done, Saint Nicholas opened the disk and let go. Instead of falling to the floor, the disc stayed aloft as if held by an invisible hand. Music sweet as could be rolled from the device. The metal began to open, unfolding outwards like an origami shape being undone. Impossibly, the tiny disk became a wondrous door. It opened and Hanna saw only stars within.

"Am I supposed to go in? Will this take me to heaven, Nick?"

He shrugged.

"But what if I end up somewhere worse?"

"Hanna Bear," Saint Nicholas said, taking her by the paw. "If works are love to be done on earth, then certainly faith is the hope by which you must tread. I said that the Big Man sent me. Trust in that."

Nodding, Hanna was just about to go through when she said, " Nick, I forgot how wonderful it is to be seen."

Saint Nicholas laughed joyfully and slapped his sides, "You were always seen, just not in the way you were used to."

Stepping within, the ghost of Hanna departed at last.

Epilogue

At last, I shall put down the pen and explore a new dream. You see, everything I have told you is real, just not where you live. Of course, if you don't know how to walk the world of dreams this will make no sense. I invite you to my world if this is a secret you would like to learn.

Sincerely, your guide in the *onraumer*,

-Fool

Postscript: Danger did eventually get Itchy Ro back, but on account of the permanent marker Apocalypse had used to paint lipstick upon it, the ball was renamed Missy Ro.

Supporting the Indie Author

Hello! I hope this story brought you on a wild and unforgettable ride. As always it was with passion and desire to share a sliver of the Good, Great, Beautiful, and True that I wrote this story. But, I cannot write when I cannot eat. While purchasing a book goes a long way to sustainably bringing you new and fresh tales, it is a thriving ecosystem that ensures this boat stays afloat.

What do I mean?

Well, one of the biggest things that helps keep food on my table is ratings or reviews. In a sea of books, this is the one thing that assuredly turns heads. The more ratings and reviews (positive & negative) the more likely new readers are willing to try out my books. It takes less than five minutes to head to Amazon or Goodreads, using the book name in the search, and clicking the number of stars you believe this story is worth. With that in mind, I must humbly ask. . . Could you please leave a rating or review?

Sincerely & With Gratitude

Izaic Y

P.S. You can stay in the know regarding future books, audio projects, book club resources, and other fun things by visiting my website at izaicyorks.com and subscribing to my newsletter.

Set Two Decades After Walktal

CYBERPUNK X BLACK MIRROR X BLADE RUNNER

An Audio Book / Drama

They took me in the dead of night. . .
well not just me, there were others,
but most are gone now. They took
us to a deep, deep place. The kind
with magic, where only the Tallmen
and fairies go. They beat us, they
starved us, they took our minds,
and broke our souls. . . well, most
anyways. I survived and this is my
tale. . .

Set Two Decades

Before "Ascendant"

THE LAND IS BREAKING…

THE MAGIC IS SICK…

THE DRAGONS ARE DEAD…

Left with few choices,
Magnate Rivia has placed
all hope in a curious invalid
and a foolish expedition. Not
only to discover new lands but
for the invalid's father's sake, who has
been imprisoned for falsity under oath.
Namely, claiming that the world of
Aithos is a globe. Should the expedition
fail, Magnate Rivia will have no choice,
but rebel against the High King himself.

COMING TO KICKSTARTER MARCH 2024
RELEASING NOVEMBER 2024

Learn About All Upcoming Projects at izaicyorks.com
OR

Also By Reading Order

Saga of Valor Series

    1. *Ascendant: Saga of Valor*

    2. *Walktall* (Novella set 20 years prior to *Ascendant*)

The Leosan And Cloistered

    1. *Aithos* (Kickstarter March 2024 & Launching November 2024)

Stand Alone

- *The Redline* (Free wherever podcasts are found *or* at izaicyorks.com)

- *Does A Snowflake Make a Sound*

Support and shop from *izaicyorks.com*

Why buy from my store? Simple, I make more money than what Amazon or other major retailers allow. For example, purchasing *Ascendant* from amazon earns about 0.90 cents, while I make the full 4.99 from my personal store.

Thanks for the support!

About Izaic

Although he was born in Detroit, Michigan, the Army brought the Yorks family to Tacoma, Washington in Izaic's younger years. Until a move to Hillsborough, North Carolina, he'd considered the Pacific Northwest his one and only home. His story in the sport of running has a different beginning than most of his colleagues as he didn't participate in athletics until high school, often choosing theater and musical interests over sports. It was not until he watched the 2008 Olympics with his physically disabled sister that he decided to pursue track—eventually leading to a career as a professional athlete.

Izaic's passions however do not stop at the track but also extend into that of stories and writing. Izaic always knew he wanted to write novels but it was recently that he decided to dive in headfirst, after all every journey begins with a single step. He has spent years training and competing; and when he is not training he is dedicating countless hours to his passion of storytelling, writing fantastical stories, enjoying time with his family, and playing the occasional Dungeons and Dragons game.

Izaic likes to think of himself as a natural-born storyteller having loved sharing stories from a young age. He thrives when he is able to express his creativity through writing or spoken narrative, bringing his audience to new worlds. Izaic believes in writing stories that uplift and leave the readers filled with hope and seeking Virtue. He dedicates intentional time to perfecting the art of storytelling through regularly writing new stories, acting out new characters, and sharing his unique ideas with his wife who is sure to help him nix all the bad ones.

Learn More at izaicyorks.com

You can find Izaic's full-length high fanta-sy novel for purchase at his website. If you get the chance a rating and reviews go a long way towards putting food on the table!